KU-369-093

Milly Molly ®

B O O K S

This Milly Molly book belongs to

_____

For my grandchildren

Thomas, Harry and Ella

Milly Molly and Grandpa's Oak Tree

Copyright © Milly Molly Books, 2001

Gill Pittar and Cris Morrell assert the moral right to
be recognised as the author and illustrator of this work.

All rights reserved. No part of this book may be
reproduced or utilised in any form or by any means,
electronic, or mechanical, including photocopying,
recording, or by any information storage or
retrieval system without the prior written permission
of the publisher.

Published by
Milly Molly Books
P O Box 539
Gisborne, New Zealand
email: books@millymolly.com

Printed by Rhythm Consolidated Berhad, Malaysia

ISBN: 0-9582208-7-5

10   9   8   7   6   5   4   3   2   1

WITHDRAWN FROM STOCK

Central A...
Douglas: 4...
St Mary's

Milly, Molly
and
Grandpa's Oak Tree

"We may look different
but we feel the same."

ST. MARY'S ROAD BRANCH

355473

Grandpa and Granny Peg lived on the edge
of town in a house that had been there for eve

In their garden grew the biggest oak tree
Milly and Molly had ever seen.
"My oak tree is one hundred years old,"
said Grandpa. "And by Granny Peg's reckoning,
we'll soon be one hundred years old too."

Grandpa and Granny Peg belonged to everyone. Everyone had enjoyed a pot of strawberry jam from Granny Peg's pantry.

And everyone's woodshed had been given
a barrow of Grandpa's firewood during
moments of hardship.

Everyone, especially Milly and Molly,
loved Grandpa and Granny Peg.

One day Grandpa woke up after a good night's sleep and still felt sleepy. Milly and Molly were very surprised to find him still in bed on a sunny day.

When Granny Peg suggested they fetch Doctor Smiley, they ran as fast as their little legs would take them.

"Now there's nothing to worry about,"
Doctor Smiley comforted Granny Peg.
"Grandpa is wearing out. It's time he went
a little slower."

But when Granny Peg went back to her kitchen Doctor Smiley kindly said to Grandpa, "You must prepare for Granny Peg's future. You may not see another winter but she could live to be one hundred."

Grandpa leapt out of bed. Milly and Molly
and Granny Peg knew better than to argue
with Grandpa and besides they were
relieved to see him back to his old self.

By the end of the day Grandpa's woodshed was full of firewood and Milly and Molly had made a stack of all the small bits for kindling.

By the end of the next day Grandpa had filled
the pantry with jam from the strawberries
in his garden and Milly and Molly had labelled
all the jars.

The day after, all the pumpkins were in tidy rows. While Grandpa stacked the top shelf, Milly and Molly stacked the bottom shelf.

And the day after that, Grandpa had bagged
all his potatoes and given Milly and Molly
each a pocketful of little ones to take home
for their dinner.

The next day Milly and Molly found Grandpa
sitting under his oak tree with a basket
full of acorns.

"Look," he said, "who would believe that this little fellow could grow into a mighty oak tree."

"Can we plant acorns in our gardens?" Milly and Molly asked.

"You certainly can," said Grandpa.

"Promise me you will water them and look after them and one day you will have oak trees of your own to sit under."

Grandpa had one last chore to do before he hopped into bed. He wrote:

My dear Granny Peg,
There are enough pumpkins, potatoes and firewood to last you until you are one hundred and there's enough strawberry jam for everybody. Please put me under the oak tree and I will wait for you there. Love from Grandpa.

The next morning he had gone.

One day a town planner came to visit.
"Granny Peg," he said, "the council would
like to cut down your tree and move your
house to make way for a new highway."
"I won't leave Grandpa," said Granny Peg.
"He can go too," said the town planner.
"Oh no he can't," said Granny Peg.
"He's waiting for me under the oak tree."

Fortunately the town planner was a tree lover. He agreed Grandpa and his oak tree should not be disturbed. Granny Peg thanked the town planner for being so understanding and gave him a pot of strawberry jam.

Grandpa's calculations were perfect.
Granny Peg enjoyed her hundredth birthday
and before she hopped into bed she put
the last piece of firewood on her fire.

The next morning she too had gone.

Granny Peg had only just been reunited
with Grandpa under the oak tree when
the bulldozer moved in.

CITY
LIBRARY
CORK

If your highway kinks around a very old tree, it may well be Grandpa's oak tree. And if you find an acorn, plant it in your garden. Water it and take care of it and one day you too will have an oak tree of your own to sit under.

Milly Molly

B O O K S

Other picture books in the Milly Molly values series include:

- Milly and Molly's Monday   ISBN 1-877297-06-2

- Milly Molly and What Was That?   ISBN 0-9582208-1-6

- Milly Molly and Beefy   ISBN 0-9582208-3-2

- Milly Molly and Jimmy's Seeds   ISBN 0-9582208-2-4

- Milly Molly and Taffy Bogle   ISBN 0-9582208-4-0

- Milly Molly and Oink   ISBN 0-9582208-5-9

- Milly Molly and BushBob   ISBN 0-9582208-6-7

www.millymolly.com